AC... F

M ...

ACE, KING OF MY HEART

An Assateague Pony's Tale of Strength and Survival

LEA HERRICK

Ace, King of My Heart
By Lea Herrick

Summary: Ace, a tiny, wild colt born on Assateague Island, struggles to survive (with a little help from his animal friends) as he grows into a magnificent stallion.
[1. Assateague pony-Fiction. 2. Ponies-Fiction.
3. Assateague Island-Fiction.]

ISBN 10: 1535022035
ISBN 13: 9781535022033

Library of Congress Control Number: 2016911068
CreateSpace Independent Publishing Platform
North Charleston, South Carolina

2DogNitePress

TABLE OF CONTENTS

ACKNOWLEDGMENTS

Thank you to the Assateague Island Alliance, the Assateague Coastal Trust, the Friends of the Assateague State Park, and the Assateague State & National Seashore Park Rangers, who work tirelessly to preserve the Maryland portion of this beautiful island and its wildlife.

A special thanks to National Seashore Park Superintendent Debbie Darden and Ranger Liz Davis. In a meeting on a cold January morning, they portrayed the Seashore's 50th Birthday so wonderfully that it spurred me to write a story to pique the wonder and curiosity of the child in all of us.

The books of Dr. Ronald Keiper, William R. Wroten, Jr., and Andrea Jauck & Larry Points were invaluable in researching the island's history, habitats and behaviors of the wild horse society on Assateague. Thank you, Liz and Rene, for pointing me in the direction of those books.

Rene Capizzi, your enthusiasm for this project was contagious, and your suggestion of the storyline was superb!

National Park Rangers Allison Turner and Kelly Taylor, words cannot express the gratitude for the work you do with the horses.

Thanks to Nora Howell for her beautiful illustrations and to Krystal Colon for her terrific assistance with the final artwork. Mi querida Lucia - muchas gracis por el dibujo de los delfines.

To my husband, who never tired of driving me to the island to "see the ponies" and some of whose photographs served as templates for the illustrations and cover in *Ace, King of My Heart* – thank you.

DEDICATION

Ace, King of My Heart is dedicated to the wild ponies of Assateague. May they live forever free!

INTRODUCTION

As we celebrate the 50th Birthday of Assateague Island National Seashore and the 100th Anniversary of the National Park Service, we look to the "Seventh Generation Principle" of the Native Americans who lived in harmony with the world around them. This principle states that we must consider in every decision how it will impact the next seven generations to come.

Assateague Island essentially remains as it was in the time of our ancestors and is one of the last remaining pristine environments on the Atlantic Seaboard, unspoiled by human development and the pressures of an ever-growing population. What makes this island even more notable is its society of wild horses that roam freely on the Maryland portion of the barrier island. Dedicated individuals have studied the herd and found them to have a complex family structure. These horses eat, sleep, so-cialize and raise their young on Assateague, and life for them is a daily struggle. *Ace, King of My Heart* is just one story of one pony living on Assateague, his fragile island home.

LH
2016

*"Wild Creatures, Like Men,
Must Have a Place to Live."*

(RACHEL CARSON, 1943)

Part 1

A NEW LIFE ON THE ISLAND

Once upon a time, thousands of years ago, glaciers collided and waves pounded in the sea.

As if by magic, a tiny, windswept barrier island was born in the Atlantic off the coast of a place called Maryland.

This was a land of legends where Indians roamed, Spanish/European explorers visited and pioneers homesteaded. This was "Assateague," the marshy place across, so named by the Native Americans who lived on the island between the ocean and the Sinepuxent Bay.

This island home is shared by many of nature's creatures. Each and every animal, fowl and plant species is truly a miracle in its own right. The largest of these is a herd of wild horses, or as they are more commonly known, the ponies of Assateague, although there is nothing ordinary or common about these beautiful animals.

Stories abound of Spanish galleons that were ship-wrecked off the coast of Assateague during hurricanes and nor'easters, carrying horses aboard that had to swim to shore. These horses, fighting tumultuous wind and waves, clung to life in a desperate attempt to survive, finally making it safely to this barrier island.

Other tales are of pirates coming ashore, burying treasure and stashing horses for their return after plunderous voyages, but never to be seen or heard from again nor ever reclaiming their mares and stallions.

Yet another local folklore suggests that early colonists hid their domesticated horses and other livestock on Assateague to avoid paying taxes on the animals. Over time, these horses became wild and feral, having to adapt to withstand the brutal winters and harsh summer heat.

Whatever you choose to believe, know this – the Assateague ponies are magnificent creatures who have been here for over three hundred years and belong here to be wild and free forever.

This is not the end of the story; in fact, it is just the beginning, for life is constantly renewing itself. This is part of the great plan for all species.

The cycles of nature are endless, and winter is a time of sleep and rest for many. Tucked between the sand dunes along the beaches of the Atlantic Ocean and the salt marshes of the Sinepuxent Bay is the quiet solitude of the loblolly pine forests of Assateague. The end of February was near, and the delicate long green needles of the pines glistened as the sun cast its rays on the snow covered branches. Beneath the trees, a deep layer of pine needles blanketed the forest floor that dampened almost any sound. In the scrubby underbrush, a band of seven ponies was moving about, grazing on bayberry bushes, crunching the stems with their powerful teeth and savoring every last morsel.

The days were growing longer and the nights shorter as February turned to March, and there was more than a hint of springtime in the air. One of the mares in the band pulled away from the other horses, and her stallion was noticeably nervous, attempting to keep the other mares and yearlings together. As evening fell, the mare found a special spot all to herself. Another miracle of Assateague occurred – a beautiful, new foal was born and made his first appearance in a cold and unfamiliar world.

His mother, Queenie, had exquisite pinto markings of chestnut and white, and his father, Jack, was a deep charcoal color like the midnight sky. This precious colt opened his eyes for the first time and could barely stand while his long spindly legs wobbled about. He tried to make sense of this strange and eerie place. Then he set his eyes on his mother and gingerly walked toward her, searching for the warmth of Queenie's nuzzle and the creamy taste of a mother's milk. After a short while, the foal's thirst was quenched, and when his eyes began to grow heavy, he lay down on a bed of soft pine needles and drifted off for a lengthy nap.

All newborns are adorable, and this colt was no exception. He had a coat of one color – a rich, milk chocolate brown, with a cinnamon tail and mane. His only other marking was a striking white patch in the shape of a little leaf or spade, centered perfectly on his forehead below his ears and right above his big brown eyes.

After about an hour, he awakened and again looked for his mother, Queenie. She was close by and decided it was high time that he had a name. His tiny white marking on his forehead stood out against the brown background of his scraggly, furry coat. In the darkness, she neighed and called him "Ace," because he looked like he had a miniature ace, like that on a deck of cards, right smack dab in the middle of his head. Ace instinctively understood this horse language and stood up. Still somewhat unsteady on his feet and a bit knock-kneed, he made his way toward Queenie for another quick snack of milk.

Ace nickered and neighed and didn't want to let Queenie out of his sight while he ate and slept throughout the night. Queenie never took her eyes off Ace because he was imprinting on her heart.

The dawn of a new day brought strength and the excitement of adventure as Ace explored his new world on this his first full day of life. After breakfast, dining on his usual meal, of course, the little colt decided to play. Ace galloped around and around his mother in a circle, jumping over small plants, with his little legs growing more assured of each step and stride he took. Ace threw his muzzle up into the air and whinnied in sheer playful joy and delight. Queenie kept a watchful eye on Ace, for he began to venture farther away in his eagerness to see what lie ahead. Oh, there was so much to investigate, and Ace was a curious colt, so he set out to see what he could find.

He picked up a pinecone with his mouth and repeatedly tossed it high above his head. That was great entertainment, and Ace amused himself for quite some time with this antic.

It was still quite chilly on this March morning, but the sun was up and felt so toasty warm against a newborn's coat. Ace didn't get too far before his mother, Queenie, gave a little nicker. She walked toward Ace and gently nudged him along as they slowly made their way back to the band of horses in the woods.

This was all very intriguing for Ace. He had never seen anyone but his mother before, and admittedly, he was a bit frightened of the others. Queenie seemed to know all the ponies that gathered around in amazement, checking out this new, tiny colt. Ace started to feel rather intimidated - other mares and their yearlings came closer and closer, and then the huge, handsome dark stallion Jack approached, towering over him. He was an imposing figure. Suddenly, Queenie placed herself between Ace and Jack in a very protective stance, and Jack backed off just as Queenie was getting ready to give him a swift kick with her hind legs. Why, Ace now was feeling his oats, so to speak. He extended his head toward the stallion, with his ears erect, opening and closing his mouth so rapidly that it appeared as though Ace was wildly champing. How hilarious it looked, but the little foal was very proud of himself. His mother began to calm down and moved nearer to Jack but kept a distance from the rest of the horses after this first encounter. Jack laid his head on the back of Queenie's neck ever so softly. Could this stallion be his father?

These mares and their offspring must be his aunts and cousins, for they are part of the family band, too. The stallion and the mares all looked after the yearlings and each other, and Ace was so happy to be a member of this group. It took the entire band to watch over and raise the young properly, and they depended on one another for survival and protection.

Ace felt very secure and once again dozed off to sleep. There had been so much activity that day, tiring the little colt, but the drama was not over yet.

Jack stayed alert and could always sense when danger was afoot because foxes on the island would search for a weak or sick foal. Sure enough, that evening a red fox circled in the brush at dusk and spied Ace. You could see the white tip of the fox's tail in the moonlight while he lurked in the bushes. In an instant, Jack caught the fox's scent.

The stallion lowered his head with his ears pressed back, snaking his way through the thickets. He ran toward his mares, nipping at their back legs and heels, herding them and their offspring through the forest with Queenie leading the way. Ace was beside her and galloped as fast as his little legs would carry him, doing his best to keep up with his mother and the others. All you could hear were the snorts and heavy breathing of these animals when they charged ahead in the twilight. Their steamy breaths crystallized in the cold air while they raced through the night. Jack brought up the rear in constant vigilance, guarding his family. He was a good father, and he would not rest until all were where they were supposed to be. The fox was no match for the stallion, and it stealthily moved away just when the band headed to safety over the dunes.

The crisis was averted, and things seemed to be going very peacefully with the days and weeks shifting gradually into spring. But, as it so often happens in life, sometimes there is a little glitch. What you do with these glitches helps to make you who you are.

Part 2

THE INNOCENCE OF A COLT

Ace was the only colt born that March, and he came into this world earlier than all the other foals that season. The newborns arrived later in the spring and into the summer, making Ace the in-between baby. His cousins the yearlings were almost an entire year older while his newborn cousins were several months younger. Ace continued to stay close by his mother, but he liked to play with the yearlings and the new colts although some of them could be a little rough. Ideally, as long as Ace had his mother, Queenie, and his father, Jack, to watch over him, he felt very content.

Ace spent the springtime among his band while they grazed on the salt marshes beside the coastal bay. The breezes there were lovely and ever so gentle. The cordgrass was tough and chewy, and rather salty, but Ace would make due. His newly formed teeth were beginning to chomp through all kinds and manner of things, even poison ivy. He loved those berries and leaves, and though people need to avoid that vine because they will itch and scratch all over, it didn't bother Ace in the least. Truthfully, he viewed it as a kind of a delicacy and scrumptious treat. The taste was better in winter, but Ace didn't care. He was devouring every last mouthful of it. He still was consuming his mother's milk. That

would go on for quite some time, as he wasn't very inter-
ested in the freshwater ponds on the island...why should
he be when he could partake of Queenie's delicious food.
It was so much healthier and helped Ace to build up his
resistance to many illnesses and diseases that could cause
little ponies to perish. Mother Nature always has a plan.
This plan was for Ace to drink mom's formula for almost
the entire first year of his life and to thrive and be the
strongest and healthiest colt any colt could possibly be.

The high marshes of the island were like a wonderful pasture of salt meadow hay, and Ace was taking in all
the sights and sounds of Assateague. All creatures great
and small fascinated him, especially the brown-headed
cowbirds and cattle egrets who would take turns hitch-
ing a ride on the older ponies' backs as they traveled
throughout the island. It was a common occurrence to

see the cowbirds strutting up and down the ponies' necks and withers, searching for whatever may be hiding in the horses' beautiful, thick manes. The large, white egrets with their long, yellow legs and beaks and the cowbirds with their glossy black bodies help the ponies by picking off the bugs from their coats. They love to dine and feed on these insects while the horses are thrilled to assist with the ride, for these birds rid the ponies of pesky, nuisance critters, like lice, ticks, and flies. Ace, however, preferred to try to play with the egrets as they pranced about on the ground around him. Ace would paw the earth and charge after the birds, hoping against hope that they would run around in circles with him, playing a great game of chase since he really just wanted a friend. Unfortunately, the egrets would fly away or alight on another pony's back because they didn't have time for such childish and foolish pranks.

Assateague is teeming with new life in the springtime, and many species love the island. Diamondback terrapins slowly crawl their way with their webbed feet from the wet tidal mud ready to lay their eggs on a sandy shore. These turtles are skittery and tuck their heads and legs back inside their shells at the first sign of danger. They wait and then march on until they reach just the right spot to bury and deposit their eggs. A couple of months later, the hatchlings will be ready to make their trek back to the water. All at once, they will wriggle and dig their way out of the hole, instinctively following the path generations of turtles have taken as they head back to the bay.

Migrating birds and ducks are visiting the estuaries around Sinepuxent Bay, and it is like a wonderful nursery for them to raise their young. Osprey, or sea hawks, busily prepare nests of sticks, driftwood and seaweed high atop channel markers in preparation for the arrival of their new chicks. The osprey will use these nests year after year for each new brood to come.

Some residents live on Assateague year round. In the late spring and early summer, it is standard to see baby mallard ducklings, with their soft, yellow and brown puffs of down, swimming in a line behind mother duck. Mom quacks and squawks if the babies get too far away from her. The beautiful Canada geese also have their little, beige goslings swimming about in a tight-knit group, with mama goose leading the way and papa goose bringing up the rear. The mother and father goose stay together forever, like the osprey, raising many young in the seasons ahead. All the new babies of Assateague are truly a sight to behold! What could be more perfect?

Spring turned into summer and with the change of seasons came the broiling afternoon heat of the noonday sun. The band of ponies left the marsh as it was just too buggy, and they all moved to the beach in single file fashion, led by Queenie, to enjoy the sea breezes. The wind helped to shoo the biting flies away from the horses and provided them with relief from the high temperatures and humidity on the island. The ponies swished their tails like giant fly swatters, fanning themselves and munching on the beach dune grasses in the late afternoon sun.

Ace loved all the smells of the ocean, and his nostrils could not take in enough of that salty sea air. He would sniff and snuff and he particularly delighted in jostling seashells with his hooves to see what was inside them. He would pick up little pieces of driftwood that floated ashore and would flip them into the air, embracing his favorite pastime once again.

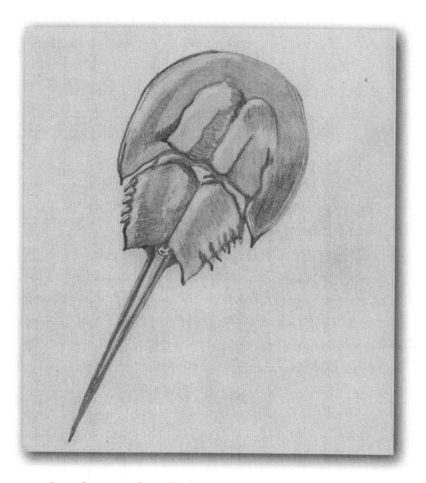

One day, Ace found a horseshoe crab that had washed up in the tide. It looked so big and strange to him, like something from prehistoric days with its reddish-brown, horseshoe-shaped shell and weird, pointy tail. Was it a spider? a crustacean? a sea creature? Unquestionably, this object was from another time and place. Ace inquisitively bumped it with his frisky feet and was especially careful to keep it right side up, as he really did not wish to harm it. The horseshoe crab is very important to both man and many shorebirds' survival. It was like a little game until he grew tired of it.

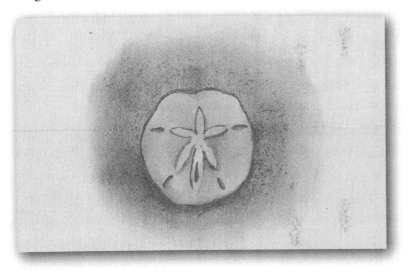

The horses stood on the beach for what seemed an eternity. The great black-backed gulls and terns soared in the air, landing close to the ponies' feet, looking for mollusks to eat. They probed the pink whelks with their bills, and laughing gulls cackled with delight. A lone herring gull meandered up to the bleached skeleton of a sand dollar and came up empty handed. Nothing to eat there and it's no wonder since some believe these sand dollars are indeed the lost coins of the mermaids or the people of Atlantis. Finally, the gull found a starfish on the sand and feasted on it.

Gray willets flashed their black and white wings as they ran all about the shore. They were hoping to grab a dinner of the mole crabs that were there in front of them scurrying one minute and would then disappear into the soft, wet sand when the tide came in the next.

All of a sudden, the horses waded straight into the ocean, hanging out just where the waves began to break. Then abruptly they turned and let the waves wash over their backs with the sea spray shooting over their heads and manes. Even Ace got into the act and stood close to his mother, never wanting to be too far from her. Oh, how refreshing this was, and Ace couldn't remember having this much fun before. The waves washed over and over them again and again. Why, these ponies were probably the first surfers and horseplay abounded. What a great way to cool off and lose those miserable, green-headed flies.

It was getting to be dinnertime, and you can always tell when that is at the beach. A pod of dolphins swam together in a straight line, not too far from shore. Their sleek, gray bodies were bounding up and down, in and out of the waves, with their skin shimmering in the sunshine in the late afternoon sky. Some of the younger dolphins jumped out of the water and did acrobatic flips in the air, having a riotous time as they traveled parallel to the shoreline. Overhead, several brown pelicans with their long, pointy beaks and their vast, flapping wings were flying back to their nesting roosts while they looked for supper. Occasionally, one of the pelicans would nose dive straight into the ocean, beak first, and come up with a fish for dinner (perhaps an Atlantic Menhaden), which disappeared quickly into his large, expandable pouch. The pelicans have keen eyesight and certainly don't need any spectacles or eyeglasses! Wouldn't they look comical, though if they did?

The horses decided to come ashore, walking back onto the warm sand; without warning, one by one, they lay down and started rolling on their backs from side to side. Then they promptly all stood up and were nice and clean and dry from their little dip in the ocean.

The sun was just beginning to set, and the colors of the sky were the most resplendent coral and turquoise. The breeze had changed course and was coming off the ocean once again. You could hear the waves lapping on the shore when the tide went in and out, and the gulls cried as they soared back over the water. If ever there was perfection, this hour on the beach was it with nature giving the best it had to offer in this island setting. This is truly the treasure of Assateague – pirates' bounty of gold and silver cannot compare to the beauty that abounds on the shores of Maryland!

Part 3

§

ADVERSITY OF ADOLESCENCE

L ife seemingly could have gone on forever like this, but as the days grew shorter, it became evident that summer was coming to a close and autumn was not far behind. Ace stayed with Queenie, Jack and the other ponies in the band, and while the new foals of that season grew larger, Ace attempted to play with them more and more. They would frolic and play-fight with each other, nipping and biting and cow kicking with their hind legs as they tried to crawl on one another's backs. This could go on for hours, and even though they were just horsing around, sometimes it could get a bit hairy. When that happened, Ace would drop to his knees in a turtle posture, pulling his legs beneath him. Some of the colts and

fillies could be a bit snippy and would pull Ace's mane and tail with their teeth until Ace ran away. Then the foals would stop and run over to Queenie or one of the aunts to pester them for a while. Queenie would tolerate the roughhousing for a bit but when she needed to rest, she would show her displeasure by lashing her tail, and the youngsters knew to stop their hijinks.

Ace didn't really resemble his cousins because all the new ponies in the band had coats of several colors with markings of white, mahogany and red. Ace looked somewhat like his father, but he had not yet grown into the majestic appearance that gave Jack that exceptional air of grandeur. He felt like the odd pony out, looking a bit different and maybe even a little homely now, and he was just out of step with the other colts and fillies in the band.

Ace tried to remain positive and basked in the fleeting warmth of the autumn sunshine. As the band of horses moved back into the marsh, the island was filled with migrating monarch butterflies feeding on the plentiful goldenrod while they made their pilgrimage south to Mexico, thousands of miles away. Oh, what a spectacular sight these monarchs were in their dazzling splendor of orange, black and white, like jeweled wings a flight throughout the air. It was also time for some of the waterfowl to leave, moving southward to avoid the frigid temperatures of the Atlantic winter. While the ponies looked to the sky, they heard the deafening chorus and

honking of the snow geese, and the heavens were covered with thousands of white birds flying in a "V" formation. Ace stood out on the mud flats. When it was very silent, some of the geese in taking flight were so low that he could hear the wind beneath their black-tipped wings as they flapped and flew over the marsh. If you have never heard that sound, then you have truly missed out on something extraordinary that only a few can say they have experienced.

Days turned into weeks and the weeks into months as time passed. Ace continued to grow and to flourish, and it was almost impossible to believe that an entire year had already gone by because Ace had now had his second birthday!

Autumn approached once again, and the colt could not shake the feeling that change was in the air, more than just the turning of the seasons. One day, he was grazing with his family on salt meadow hay when Jack appeared from the tall grass and unexpectedly charged toward him. Jack's ears were pinned flat to his head, his nostrils pulled tight; with his teeth bared, he bit Ace on the back. Then the stallion reared up on his hind legs. When he came down with his hooves - inches from Ace's head with eyes all a fury - it sounded like thunder as Jack's feet crashed to the earth. Ace was petrified and didn't know what to do. Why was his father attacking him? What had he done to deserve this? Jack struck again and again, biting and hitting, screaming into the air with his mighty jaws wide open. Ace was no contender for the fierce stallion. Then he remembered that the young colts had, had play fights, and now he understood. This was in preparation for the day when he would have to leave his family band and go out on his own because there was room for only one stallion. Ace, having come of age, was now perceived as a threat to his father, Jack. He loved his parents and all his relatives, but the little colt realized what he had to do. He turned and sorrowfully took one last look at his family and at his beloved mother. Then with his tail hanging low, he stole off through the brush in the evening shadows, alone for the first time in his life. Queenie watched with longing eyes as her son disappeared into the night while Ace left the little pony band forever.

Part 4

Part 4

A SOLITARY LIFE

W inter was again upon the island. Ace had to learn to fend for himself, which was no easy task in the stormy weather. The wind howled and the sands blew, and at times, the freezing rain and snow seemed to be coming down sideways in torrents. On days and nights like this, Ace took refuge in the maritime forest, not venturing too far. He would sleep standing up, locking his knees in place with his tail to the wind. He was almost three years old, and thankfully, Ace was a resourceful little pony and had learned his lessons well. He knew where all the watering holes and fresh-water ponds were in the woods on Assateague, and he would drink and drink to wash away the salty taste from his briny diet. His considerable thirst caused his belly to look a bit bloated, but wouldn't your tummy look that way, too, if you had that much salt in your food? Ace's coat had grown thick and shaggy, and this kept the colt very warm while he wandered the island with a sense of sadness and loneliness that seemed unbearable at times. The haunting, mournful call of the loons at night only served to remind Ace of his solitude. When those feelings would almost overtake him, he remembered his mother's loving face, and he knew that he always carried a part of her heart with him.

Ace was a very sweet-natured pony, so in the winter days ahead, he made new friends on the island. Sammy, the little Sika deer, was actually a miniature elk, with short compact dainty legs. He was shy and very cute and had white spots running parallel all down his tawny brown back with a white crescent patch circling his rump. Sammy would see Ace at the ponds as they sipped water together in the evening moonlight. Sometimes Ace would break the ice for Sammy with his hoof when the watering hole had frozen over, and Sammy was most grateful for Ace's help. They shared some of the same dining tastes of poison ivy and bayberry stems and occasionally crossed paths in areas of similar habitat in the marshy wetlands and the clearings of dense understory thickets of the woodland forest. Earlier that fall, Ace noticed that Sammy loved to rub the velvet from his antlers on low-hanging bushes, and Ace decided this must be a pretty good way to scratch the itch that little ponies sometimes had. He recalled seeing the horses in his former band grooming each other, but since he didn't have any other ponies to play with, he thought this trick he learned from Sammy was fairly nifty. Ace would sidle up to branches and rub his fur against them, and it felt oh, so good! Sammy's winter coat had also grown thicker, so Ace was not alone in his shaggy appearance.

Ronnie, the raccoon, looked the part of a true bandit with his black, furry mask around his eyes contrasting against his white face. His bushy ringed tail had alternating light and dark rings surrounding it, and his ears were slightly cupped, listening for sound. Raccoons were first discovered in the New World by the expedition of Christopher Columbus, and in the Powhatan Indian language, raccoon means, "the one who rubs, scrubs and scratches with its hands." The raccoon's dense underfur insulated Ronnie from the cold chill of winter, and he would scurry and scamper about in the nighttime searching for crustaceans or whatever he could find to eat. Ronnie was very intelligent and dexterous with his front paws and long finger-like digits. He could even climb trees, catching a woodcock one evening for dinner as Ace watched in wonder and marveled at how agile this critter was. Typically, Ace would see Ronnie on the mud flats while this raccoon fished near the edge of the bay, washing and scrubbing his catch of the day before eating it. Even though there was not a lot of interaction between the two of them, it was somewhat comforting just to know that Ronnie was there and that Ace had company in the solitary winters of Assateague.

It was an altogether different matter with Ollie, the river otter. He was very elusive, and Ace played a little game trying to see if he could catch sight of this otter in his travels throughout the island. Sometimes this was very hard to do because Ollie burrowed close to the water's edge and his den had many tunnel openings to hide in. Ollie had a thick, water-repellent coat of brownish-black fur, a long tapered tail and short, muscular legs with webbed toes that helped him swim in the tidal creeks of Assateague. His flat head with a broad muzzle, long whiskers and tiny upright ears made his sense of smell and hearing very acute. The otter's large molars were useful in crushing the shells of mollusks, but his favorite diet was all manner and types of fish. Ollie was a playful chap, and although Ace rarely saw him, Ace always knew when he was about. He would see tracks in the snow where Ollie had slid down the bank, using an opening in the ice to dive into the brackish waters to fish, and Ace would hear the sound of the splash. Ollie, the otter, could hold his breath underwater for several minutes at a time, swimming out of sight and ending up in another spot in the marsh beyond eyeshot of Ace.

Another furtive creature was Chloe the cottontail, and she was a very dear little bunny rabbit. Chloe had grayish fur, long ears and large hind feet, and her most outstanding feature was her fluffy, white cottontail that looked just like a soft, puffy cotton ball! She loved to browse at night on grasses, bark and twigs on the edge of the woods. Chloe would listen with her big ears and watch with her large eyes to be on the lookout for any signs of danger or predators. Her little, brown nose would wiggle and twitch. Chloe would remain frozen in her posture, not moving a muscle for a very long time in order to blend in with her surroundings, tricking many a hunter into believing that no one was there. If Chloe sensed a threat, she could outrun most of the animals, fleeing in a zigzag pattern with speeds of up to eighteen miles per hour! How fast she was, and Ace was very impressed with this feat. Ace saw her most evenings as they chewed and nibbled on the winter vegetation. Occasionally you could hear the "Hoo H'hoo" calls of the great horned owls, and Chloe knew she needed to be extra careful when she heard those sounds and remain hidden from sight in the tall phragmites reeds. She would not be alone there because the red-winged blackbirds, with their brilliant red bars on their wings, liked to call the phragmites their home.

Oscar, the great horned owl, is very reclusive, and he is a nighttime hunter that strikes from above. Native Americans admired the great horned owl for its strength, courage and beauty, and some tribes believed owls were reincarnations of slain warriors who fly about in the night.

Other American Indians adorned facial masks made of the wing and tail feathers of the great horned owl. Still others used the feathers to make arrows because they thought these feathers gave the arrows their silence as they sped through the night toward their targets.

Oscar was large and barrel-shaped with an enormous head and feathered facial discs surrounding his immense, cat-like yellow eyes. Oscar even looked a bit cross-eyed, but don't let that fool you as his eyesight was as good as a pair of fine binoculars. There were feather tufts that stood up on his forehead resembling horns or ears, and his body was darkly barred to provide camouflage. A white patch of feathers on his throat continued like a streak running down the middle of his breast, and his wings were ever so broad. Feathers ran all the way down his legs and feet to his powerful talons and claws. Oscar was quite a remarkable sight and was a flawless hunter!

The owl's track record was broken that night because several of his prey outwitted him this day. The northern bobwhite - a roundish ground-dwelling quail with patterned feathers of brown, buff and black and a bold white and black striped head - crouched and froze, blending into the marsh. He knew better than to whistle his "bob-WHITE" call that evening as undoubtedly this would have given his location away.

Virginia the opossum, whose name comes from the Indian word meaning, "white animal," has dull grayish-brown fur all over her body, except for her white face. Opossums carry their young in their pouch, and Captain John Smith came upon these marsupials in his travels in the New World. They are famous for "playing possum" and feign death to trick their predators. At times, they can lie still for hours doing this, and tonight the opossum played a good game with Oscar and won!

In warmer months, Manny, the meadow jumping mouse, with his whiskers, long tail and kangaroo-like feet, leaps and dives into the marshy water to escape those who chase.

Part 5

UNEXPECTED COMPANIONS

It is a tough environment and only the smart and strong survive, which brings us back to Ace. The little pony was wandering the island one cold winter day, and in a clearing, he saw two other horses by themselves, grazing on saltmarsh cordgrass. He could hardly believe his eyes…they were colts just like him. In fact, they even had the shaggy coats as he did, although theirs' were a more reddish-auburn hue. Ace was apprehensive and almost afraid to approach them since the memory of that horrible hour when his father, Jack, attacked him still lingered in his mind. But, he was feeling awfully brave that day, and very lonely, and decided that nothing beats a failure like a try. Ace slowly sauntered up to the two ponies and gave a little nicker, waiting to see what their response would be.

When he drew closer, he realized that these colts were both about his size, and they looked up from their grazing, moving their bodies nearer to him. They changed stance very slightly and stood quietly together while all three investigated and sniffed each other's noses. The other ponies' ears were tilted forward, and they showed friendly interest and curiosity in Ace. They swished their tails back and forth, and it was a happy occasion. Ace was elated, and as the afternoon wore on, eating beside them, he decided he would stay with these horses. They, too, had been forced to leave their family groups and were bachelors just like he was, and the little colt was so enjoying being part of this bachelor band.

Leonard and Maynard were now Ace's new best buddies, and the three bachelors would spend the next few months having many merry moments together. When one of the ponies was thirsty, the other two would start to follow behind as the first horse began leading the way to the watering hole. Then Ace, Leonard and Maynard would all start running just as fast as their legs could carry them, and it became a great race to see who reached the water first. Oh, what hoopla it was!

Day in and day out, the three of them would cavort doing their monkeyshine, and Ace could not imagine being without his new friends. When they grew sleepy, if one pony yawned, before long the other two would yawn as well, and it was a whimsical sight to see. Then all three of them would take a little snooze. Ace, Leonard and Maynard entertained themselves in the weeks and months ahead with shenanigans and tomfoolery, having a grand old time!

The wintering flocks of dark-eyed juncos, with their beautiful, small slate-colored bodies and white breasts, were slowly beginning to disappear from Assateague as they journeyed back to their summer home in the Canadian tundra. Sometimes the juncos flew with a group of bright red cardinals, and both species of birds would forage together in the brushy open edges in the woods. The cardinals would stay on, but it was now time for them to say goodbye to their junco friends.

The ruddy ducks and red-breasted mergansers were also ready to take flight to the north and west for the summer. In the distance, you could hear the knocking and drumming of the downy woodpeckers as they drilled on the loblolly pines, looking for a mate. It was hard to catch a glimpse of them, but when they flitted by, you would see their black and white bars on their wings and red caps on their heads, and it was such a thrill!

As Assateague came full on into spring, things were going just too smoothly for Ace, and along came another one of those little glitches. Ace, Maynard and Leonard were meandering around the island going about their daily routine (grazing, watering, resting and playing), but Ace could sense that the other two colts were becoming a bit restless. They were slightly older than Ace and had grown stronger with each passing day. First Maynard wandered off; then Leonard disappeared. Where had they gone? Why had they broken up this comfortable and gregarious bachelor band? Deep down, Ace recognized there was something instinctual about the horses' leaving because it was time for each of them to search for a female and start his own band. There would be ritualized prancing as they challenged and fought other stallions, attempting to steal mares and their offspring. Sometimes these colts would be successful - sometimes they would not. By and large, it left Ace alone once again. Perhaps Ace was destined to be a solitary pony all his life, and he looked so forlorn and lost without his buddies. His heart ached for companionship, and he did not like being apart from the other horses on the island. Ace felt like he was in exile, banished from his original family band and now abandoned by his new bachelor group. What was a little pony to do?

Part 6

A STALLION EMERGES

A ce mustered up the courage and pressed on. There is no going backward in life...only forward. He tried to remain optimistic since spring was such a lovely time on Assateague brimming with new life and hope. The island was always changing and with the arrival of warmer days, the beautiful beach rose was in bloom. He especially enjoyed munching on the rose hips of that plant. It was chocked full of vitamins and was very nutritious for a little pony. This flower was such a gorgeous shade of pink and while Ace stood eating, completely engrossed in his meal, he almost did not see what came over the dune. The most enchanting, winsome little filly ambled by and stopped next to him. Ace looked up in disbelief and stood still in his tracks, not wanting to spook or frighten her away. Did he imagine this? Was this a mirage? Ace slowly got up his nerve and lumbered up to her. At that moment, the two ponies touched noses then nuzzled and snuggled together. Her elegant bronze tail waved in the breeze, and it was love at first sight! The graceful filly was a pinto pony with breathtakingly deep russet-brown and ivory markings. Her alabaster legs looked like she had stockings on her feet while her coffee-colored mane blew gently around her head, turning to a frosty snow color as it trailed down her neck and withers. Diamond was her name because she had a perfect white, diamond-shaped patch on her forehead that was similar in size to Ace's, and they were like matched emblems on a pair of playing cards. She was a very regal pony and looked like a princess, reminding Ace so much of his mother, and he was genuinely captivated! Diamond had recently left her family band and was on her own, too.

As the saying goes, "Every pot has its lid," and this filly thought Ace was the most handsome colt she had ever seen. He had come into his own and grown into a sturdy, solid horse and suddenly did not resemble a baby anymore. In reality, he was now a stunning, young stallion and looked just like his father in all his radiance and splendor! Ace melted as he gazed into Diamond's big doe eyes, and he knew that he was home now, for home is where your heart is.

Birds sang in the trees, and new life abounded on the beach, forest and bay. The many flocks of migrant shorebirds returned to the island once again, and the belted kingfishers and great blue herons fished to their hearts content. Bald eagles soared over the ocean with the wind lifting their wings toward the heavens, breaking the bonds of earth. Everything was as it should be, and all was right with the world.

Diamond never left Ace's side again. The ponies would romp, revel and have the most blissful and joyous days and nights with one another. Eventually, Diamond and Ace would start a family of their own. Ace was her king and Diamond was his queen, and they ruled their domain with all their offspring. The horses' spirits prevailed and reigned triumphantly!

The two of them spent many seasons and years together on Assateague, their island home, running wild and free forever. Ace was the King of Diamond's Heart, as he is the King of My Heart and the King of All Our Hearts, and they lived happily ever after!

EPILOGUE

Oh, Assateague, Oh, Assateague
My beautiful island home,
May thoughts of you stay near to me
Wherever I may roam.

The End

FOR FURTHER READING

The Assateague Ponies
  By Ronald R. Keiper

Assateague, Island of the Wild Ponies
  By Andrea Jauck & Larry Points

Assateague
  By William H. Wroten, Jr.

Ribbons of Sand
  By Larry Points & Andrea Jauck

Assateague Island National Seashore Trail Guides
  The Life of the Dunes Nature Trail
  The Life of the Forest Nature Trail
  The Life of the Marsh Nature Trail
  By the National Park Service, Dept. of Interior

TO FOSTER AN ASSATEAGUE HORSE, CONTACT

Assateague Island Alliance
www.assateagueislandalliance.org/

Proceeds from the Foster Horse Program help protect and manage the island's wild horses.

EDUCATIONAL ACTIVITY

How many plant and animal species can you identify on the following trails at Assateague Island National Seashore? Please be a good steward of our environment and do not remove any flora or disturb the fauna. Remember, this is their home. Please stay on the trails, keeping at least a school bus length away from the ponies and deer, leaving only your footprints on Assateague. Happy Trails! (If you cannot visit the island, record on the appropriate lists as many of the cast of characters that you are able to recall.)

Hint: You may refer back to the book if you need help remembering the names of species found at the different habitats on the Island. The Assateague Island National Seashore Trail Guides; the Assateague Island Mammals, Birds, and Seashells Check Lists; and the Assateague Island National Seashore Partners in Preservation Brochure are located at the visitor center and ranger station and might be of assistance to you.

THE LIFE OF THE DUNES NATURE TRAIL

1.

2.

3.

4.

5.

6.

7.

8.

9.

10.

11.

12.

SKETCHES

What are your favorite plants and animals on Assateague Island? Please feel free to draw your own pictures of them on these blank pages. A great way to start may be to trace seashells as you beachcomb on Assateague. (If you cannot visit the island, make sketches of the plants and animals that are in your neighborhood.)

SKETCHES

SKETCHES

SKETCHES

SKETCHES

SKETCHES

SKETCHES

SKETCHES

SKETCHES

NOTES

Please journal your thoughts about Assateague Island and its abundant wildlife on the following pages. (Do you think that we are living in harmony and balance with all creatures on the island as the Native Americans did over three hundred years ago? What can we do to ensure that Assateague remains a wild place for future generations to enjoy?)

NOTES

NOTES

NOTES

NOTES

NOTES

NOTES

NOTES

NOTES

ABOUT THE AUTHOR

Lea Herrick was born and raised in the Middle Atlantic States, living briefly in Europe as a child.

Ms. Herrick's first book, *The Courageous Corgi*, chronicled the journey of a rescued dog from Wales and his odyssey of courage in finding his "forever home." *The Courageous Corgi* is a recipient of the prestigious Mom's Choice Award, which honors excellence in family-friendly media, products and services.

Lea Herrick was inspired to write *The Courageous Corgi* and *Ace, King of My Heart* as tributes to her love for animals and the environment, with the hope that all living things will be cherished and protected. Portions of the proceeds from the sale of both books assist organizations with these endeavors.

Made in the USA
Columbia, SC
03 July 2018